The
White Stone

Pauline Lewis

Christian Focus Publications Ltd

© Pauline Lewis 1990

ISBN 1 871676 207

Published by
Christian Focus Publications Ltd
Geanies House, Fearn, Ross-shire
IV20 1TW, Scotland, Great Britain

CONTENTS

PAGE

CHAPTER ONE

The two boys felt like midgets as they stood gazing up at the great height of the temple. Built on to the original wall of rock, it towered far above them. Michael the older of the two, his dark eyes shining with pride, turned to his cousin.

'What a tremendous feat! To think that my father was one of the engineers. He was specially trained, you know, by the experts the King had sent from Tyre.'

Yes, Jonadab did know, for ever since his cousin had come to visit him he had been boasting about the part his father had played in the building of this magnificent temple. His own father was a scribe, a position of some importance no doubt, and worked within the very precincts of this glorious edifice but it didn't give him much scope to respond to his cousin's bragging.

'Think of the skill of even cutting out these great stones, but then to cement them together, wedging them into the original rock! Wonderful! Magnificent!'

Michael was getting short of words. It was the first time he had seen the finished temple, the glory of King Solomon and the wonder of all Israel. He had heard so much about it, and now he was enjoying displaying the knowledge he had gained from listening to stories of his father's exploits. Jonadab was tired of craning his neck and looked around for some diversion.

'Hey! Look, Michael! Camels!' He had caught a glimpse of them between a gap in the roofs of the house that huddled below them. He grabbed Michael's arm. 'A caravan is coming. Let's go and give them a welcome.'

The slap of their sandals on the rough stone of the narrow streets betrayed the fact that the boys were from homes of some wealth. Brightly coloured coats billowed out behind them as they careered downwards. Resisting the smell of newly baked bread as they passed through the bakers row, they had reached the tent-makers alley when Michael suddenly snatched at Jonadab's hand and pulled him into an open doorway.

'What is..' his cousin began, but he swiftly cautioned him to silence.

'We're being followed,' he whispered.

Together they peered into the street. Two girls, hair flowing, cheeks flushed from their scamper, stood hesitating, bewildered, until Joanna spied the boys lurking in the shadows.

'For shame, Michael!' she chided.

'It's you who should be ashamed,' he responded sternly. 'Why aren't you at home with Mother? Jerusalem is no place for girls to be out on their own.'

'Mother is out. She was called to go and help a neighbour who is ill,' retorted his sister. She tossed her auburn hair in defiance, adding , 'And Deborah's mother was so grateful that I had such a good brother, who would escort us to see the sights of the city.'

She smiled seraphically, aware that, yet again, she had gained a victory, for Michael's little sister had early acquired the art of getting her own way. His sensitive face flushed, his feelings were divided between chagrin at the realisation that he was being manipulated by his sister and his pleasure at seeing her friend gazing shyly at him with obvious respect and expectation.

'Come along then,' he spoke grudgingly. 'But keep close to us, for we are going outside the gates to see the caravan, and we don't want you lost.'

'We will,' chirped the girls.

It seemed that most of Jerusalem had the same intent, but the four managed to find a good viewpoint on an embankment beside the highway. A chain of camels, noses raised, long lashed eyes drooping, plodded and lurched towards the city gates.

'They'll be from Sheba,' someone volunteered, and swiftly the information accumulated as the word was passed along. 'They usually come in the Spring, and of course everyone is wanting to come to Jerusalem to trade these days.' Gradually a stirring of expectancy rippled through the crowd as they realised that this was no ordinary caravan.

'Look!' Joanna whispered, 'there is gold on those bridles.'

'Yes, and see those special seats, with curtains round them. They must be important visitors.'

But now the whisper of expectation was changing to roars of acclamation for into sight came a phalanx of warriors, ebony skinned, muscles rippling, bearing a palanquin. Even the staves for carrying it were ornately carved, and the curtains that shielded the occupant from the sun were of the finest silk, embroidered with silver thread. Joanna gasped with delight, for, as the chair was right before them, a mischievous wind lifted a corner of the curtain just enough for them to catch a glimpse of a jewelled hand and the shining tresses of the dark beauty within.

'It's the Queen! The Queen of Sheba!'

Michael held them back as the crowd surged towards the gate, for he knew he would be held responsible for the girls' safety, whether he had accepted the charge willingly or not. Joanna talked excitedly of the splendour and beauty of the royal visitor.

'But her wealth is nothing to that of our King Solomon,' Michael reminded them. 'That is why she is coming to make a treaty with him.'

'Yes indeed,' corroborated Jonadab. 'Why, no one has such wealth or riches as our King. When she sees him she will feel like a pebble from the beach before a lustrous diamond.'

'Or like a little olive before a pomegranate,' was Michael's comparison.

'Haven't you heard about the glory of King Solomon's throne?' Jonadab was in his element now. It was his chance to display his knowledge. 'Why, the Queen of Sheba will need all her courage even to approach the King when he is on his throne. My father met a man who had seen the King seated in judgment. He said it was a fearful sight. The throne is of pure gold, with seven steps. On either side are lions that are made of gold,' he explained, as the girls gasped in wonder. 'But they are as large as life, and terrible in their appearance. They say that when King Solomon ascends the throne the beasts extend their paws, but if an evil man approaches the throne the lions will lash their tails and set up a terrible roaring.'

They were by now following the crowds back into the city. As they came in through the gate Michael felt a heavy hand gripping his shoulder. He spun round to find himself gazing into the face of Abinadab, his father's steward.

'Oh, Master Michael, please go to your mother quickly. We have been looking everywhere for you. And you, Mistress Joanna,' he added as she ran up anxiously.

'Why, Abinadab, what is it? Is something wrong?'

'Yes, yes,' he stammered, as if he could hardly get the words out. It seemed to the children that a damp, dark mist was descending upon them. 'It is your father. There has been an accident, up in the mines.'

CHAPTER TWO

There was a thunder of hooves, and the little family leaving the city leapt fearfully aside, then dusted themselves down and gazed with awe after the soldiers disappearing into the distance.

'Father says we have to thank King Solomon for the highway patrol and that we are able to travel without fear of brigands,' volunteered Michael.

'That's true,' agreed his mother.'Why, I wouldn't have thought of leaving my own village like this to visit the big city when I was a girl. Though maybe that was a blessing,' she sighed.

'Why, Mother? Why do you say that?' The boy was walking close beside his mother, protective, anxious to comfort her in her grief.

'Why? Because we lived as a community. The village elders were our guardians and counsellors. I would only have had to go to them at a time like this and they would have told me what to do.' Again, a deep sigh escaped her.

Joanna, who, with her ebullient nature could not remain repressed for long,had leapt up an incline. 'Look at these crocuses, lifting their faces to the sun,' she exclaimed, and then, 'Michael, come and see. There is a shepherd taking his sheep to fresh pasture.'

But she could not remain insensitive to the sorrow they shared as a family and she slipped back to walk on the other side of her mother. It was as if the cloak of fear that was upon the parent had spread over her children, drawing them to her.

'Mother, why didn't Father stay at home with us, instead of going to the mines?' Joanna asked as they trudged along.

It was Michael, serious and dark eyed, who answered her.'You should know that, Joanna. Every man has to do some service for the state now. It is the new law King Solomon has made : one month for the King, three months at home.'

'Your father is a skilled stonemason and engineer,' her mother took up the story. 'It was an honour that he was chosen to open these new copper mines. That's how it is that we have our fine house and estate in Amwas. The King wants the new towns developed, so it was given to us in recognition of your father's services.' She paused, weeping softly.

'Mother, what is it?' queried Michael.

'Why, they say your father has a crushed foot,but I can't help wondering how badly he is hurt. If he lives, will he be able to work again? If not, who will care for the estate?'

They had left the main highway now and were on the smaller road that led out toward the coastal plain. After a while Michael broke the silence.

'Mother, if only you had let me go to the mine. I could have cared for Father, and brought him home to you.'

Jerusha put her hand on her son's shoulder.'Son,' she chided lovingly,'we have discussed this already. Abinadab agreed with me that it was best to return to Amwas. The message came there and it could be your father is already on his way home.'

She was silent for a while and Joanna slipped her arm around her mother's waist for she sensed that she was choking back the tears again. Her daughter's sympathy was her undoing though, and for few moments the little family huddled together, crying quietly.

'This isn't the valley of weeping, you know.' An old man who was passing by , broke into their grief. 'Don't you know where you are? Look around you. This is Ajalon, the valley of victory.'

Jerusha wished she could have ignored the old man, resenting his intrusion, but she had been taught to respect the elderly and knew that she must teach her children to do so.

'Forgive us, sir, for not greeting you. We did not notice you. Peace be to you. We must be on our way.'

'Nay, nay,' he gently insisted. 'The sun is high and you must rest a while before you go further. Our house is yonder. Come, sit in the shade of our fig tree while my wife fetches water for you and prepares you a morsel to eat.'

'Please, Mother,' pleaded Joanna, and they were soon resting in the grateful shade.

Michael looked around him. Yes, this was indeed the valley of Ajalon. He remembered his father telling him about the great battle that their judge Joshua had won against his enemies, how he had prayed that the sun would not set so that his enemies wouldn't be able to escape under the cover of darkness and return to trouble them again. The old man (Isaac, they learned was his name) was recounting the tale.

'I love to tell the story,' he added simply. 'You see, we all have battles of one kind or another. Maybe we don't need to pray for the sun to stand still, but the Wonderful One is still up there to help us, if we will call on Him, as Joshua did. Never forget that.'

His wife had already brought them water, and now she set a dish of fruit and some barley loaves before them. She squatted down beside them while they refreshed themselves.

'Would you care to share your troubles with us, my daughter?' the old man enquired gently. 'We could not help but see that you were in distress.'

It was Michael who told the story. When he had finished Isaac leaned across and took his wife's wrinkled hands in his.

'I believe that you have been led here,' he declared simply. 'You see these hands? There is healing in them. My wife has a knowledge of herbs and healing arts, and the Lord has used her many times. As soon as your husband is home, send for Abigail. She will come, and you will see what God will do, for He still hears the cry of His children.'

As they continued on their way the young ones were refreshed in spirit as well as in body. 'You see, Mother,' chirped Joanna, ever the cheerful one, 'God is helping us. Father will get better, you'll see.' But to her dismay this only seemed to cause the tears to well up again. 'O Mother! You believe in God. You must do.'

'Of course she does!' Michael answered sharply, springing to his mother's defence, but the woman gently began to explain.

'When I was a girl in my village in Galilee, far from here, we met every Sabbath for prayer and Bible teaching. But then I married your father and we moved out here, and life has been so different. I haven't even been able to go to the temple for the festivals. Why should God help me now, when I have forgotten Him?'

'But Mother,' chided Joanna, who was never lost for words, 'Father has always prayed with us and taught us from the law of Moses.'

'Your father, yes. But suppose he isn't able to pray?'

'O Mother!' Michael was joining in to remonstrate now. This was too much. Surely God had sent old Isaac to give them hope.

They were nearing Amwas now, but as they entered the small town they heard something that seemed to add to Jerusha's distress. It was a child crying, that was all, but it was so pitiful, like the wailing of a soul bereaved.

'It's Hannah,' said Joanna. 'Poor Hannah, she's always in trouble. Why does she cry so, Mother?'

Their mother put her arms around her children and hurried them along as if wishing to get out of earshot of the sound.

'She's crying because she's a slave. She's been taken from her parents,' she answered harshly.

They had known about Hannah before, thought Michael. Yes, it was sad. Of course it was, but why did this seem to add to their mother's distress so particularly at this time?

CHAPTER THREE

It was hard, waiting for their father's return, not knowing when, or how he would come. But there was plenty to do to keep them busy. They had servants, for it was a large household, but the children had been trained to do their share. The next morning Joanna was out with the women fetching water from the well to fill the large water jars, while Michael worked with the men on the estate. They were claiming new ground from the hillside in order to plant an olive grove. It would be many years before they could gain a harvest from it, but they must plan for future generations. This was the King's policy.

The sun was still rising when the visitors began to arrive, friends and neighbours, anxious to hear more details of the disaster at the mine, and to know if Enoch had returned. They seemed to be full of mournful pessimism - as if they were looking forward to having a good cry at the funeral, Joanna thought bitterly.

'My father will be home soon,' she informed each one defiantly as she passed among them, offering water and dried figs. 'His foot is hurt. We don't know how badly, but my father is a strong man and he has faith. He will get well.'

'Ah, poor little girl,' they lamented.

'But tell me, my girl, who is bringing your father home? You don't know? Dear me, we must see into this.' It was Shamei, their neighbour, gross in body and in spirit. He had a fine estate of his own, yet had always cast covetous eyes upon that of Enoch, but now he was pretending to be his greatest friend. He pushed his way through to their mother, Jerusha.

'My dear woman, your husband is worthy of the greatest consideration,' he gushed. ' We should not wait for the government carts to bring him. He will be shaken to pieces. I will send some of my own men to bear him back with the utmost haste, and in comfort too. No, no, my dear woman. It is nothing. I insist. It is the least a neighbour can do.'

The visitors heard, as he had meant them to, and were quick to applaud. 'Why Shamei, that's wonderful. Of course that is what should be done. Enoch is worthy of the very best.'

'There is just one small matter, though.'

Michael entered the courtyard at this point, in time to see this odious man, his arm around his mother's shoulder, gently compelling her into the inner room. 'How dare he! How dare he! Compromising my mother in this way in my father's absence!' Michael tried to push his way through to protect her but first one and then another stopped him to enquire about his father and he could not be discourteous. By the time he reached the doorway, Shamei was coming out, a gleam of satisfaction in his porcine eyes and he was thrusting something inside his fur lined robe.

'It's all right, Michael,' his mother hastened to reassure her son, for she could see his indignation. 'Shamei is good enough to send bearers to meet Father. We should thank him, shouldn't we?' she added, anxious to dispel her son's angry looks.

'Thank you, sir,' Michael responded gruffly, but he couldn't help feeling uneasy as their neighbour strutted off, like a cockerel that has just established his supremacy in the farm yard.

The days seemed long, with many anxious thoughts crowding in unbidden during the hours of waiting, but Joanna clung to the message of hope from the old man Isaac in Ajalon, and tried to remember the healing hands of Abigail his wife. Michael was working from dawn till dusk, but his ear was ever alert to hear the sound he was waiting for. It was two days later that it came.

'Michael, Father is coming.'

Joanna was waiting for him and together they ran up to the road and out of the town. They could hear a low chant from the men as they carried the litter, for singing helped them to keep up a rhythm and seemed to make the burden lighter. Each man took it in turn to sing a line and then they would all join in the refrain. It was from one of the songs of their singing King, David, 'His mercy endures for ever.'

'He's alive anyway,' breathed Michael. 'It isn't a funeral chant.'

A 'Hallooo' rang out from the bearers as they realised they were within earshot of their destination and suddenly all the children of the town were running alongside, escorting the traveller as far as the outer gate of his courtyard.

'O Father! Father!' It was Joanna who was weeping now. Joanna, the one who had remained so bright, and had been drying everyone elses' tears.

It was her mother's turn to rally them all now. 'Joanna! Come child! Fetch water for your father. Michael, help me to get your father on his bed.' She knelt and pressed her husband's wasted hand to her lips. She would not embrace him while strangers were present. 'We thank God, my husband,' was all she uttered. She turned to the bearers, arranging refreshment. Then she called her children to her and sought to comfort them. 'Don't cry! Be brave!' she whispered as she held them close.

'Father is very ill, isn't he, Mother?' sobbed Joanna.

'Yes, he is very ill. It's been a long journey and he is in great pain, but he's alive, and while there is life there is hope. We will send for the old woman, Abigail. Michael - will you go? Take Joanna with you. Make haste.'

'Of course, Mother. We'll be back with her by nightfall.'

He was gone. Jerusha turned back to look at the man who for so many years had been a tower of strength to them. He lay on the bed, weak and helpless. His face was grey and lined with pain. As for his foot - it was just a swollen mass.

CHAPTER FOUR

Wizened little mother Abigail was a woman of few words. Uttering a welcome as soon as she saw the children turn into the valley, she went into her tiny mud-built house to collect a few possessions. Then she gesticulated to a neighbour's child. Evidently she was sending a message to her husband.'She's like a mother hen fussing about,' thought Joanna, 'and now she is gathering us under her wings.'

As they set out the girl told her of their father's home-coming. Michael was quite content to leave the narration to his talkative sister.'Mother wants us to hurry,' she gasped, for they had run most of the way there. They were walking now as fast as the old woman could manage, but suddenly she paused, clambered up a hill-side and swiftly gathered some herbs. She stopped to show them to the children, pointing out the distinguishing marks so that they would recognise them again. 'Good! heal!'she mouthed, then they were slung inside her shawl and they were on their way.

Jerusha had been watching for them and ran out eagerly to welcome the visitor and lead her in to where Enoch lay on a low couch, moaning in pain. The old woman took charge, and soon had everyone in action. Joanna was sent with her mother to prepare boiling water and Michael to search for more of the healing herbs. Off with the bandages and ill prepared splints! Abinadab was called and given special instructions for new ones. It wasn't long before the foot was bathed and bound, a healing draught given to help the sufferer sleep, and all were shooed out of the room. 'Sleep! Quiet! Good broth! No worry!' She pointed her hands heavenward as if in an attitude of prayer. 'Get better! Walk!' and she was gone.

Abigail came faithfully each morning to tend her patient and each morning she expected the children to have a supply of the healing herbs for her. They had to go further and further afield to search for them. One morning they came to some land on the outskirts of the town.

'Look, Michael,' exclaimed Joanna, 'that's Hannah, the little girl we hear crying at Ben Hadad's house. Why, look, poor thing, they have sent her to gather the dung, from where the oxen have been ploughing.'

'Poor girl,' was all her brother answered, but he didn't complain when Joanna ran up to speak to her. As the moments passed however he went up to call his sister, for he didn't want the little girl to have yet another beating because of them.

'Yes Michael, I know. I'm coming now,' Joanna

assured him. She embraced the child, whose eyes filled up at the unexpected kindness They were big and dark and had the timid look of a startled fawn.

'Peace be with you, Hannah,' and then, as they were going, Joanna called after her, 'Don't forget what I told you.'

'What did you tell her?' enquired Michael as, their basket full,they made their way back to the house.

'Why, Michael, do you know what happened? Such a terrible thing! Hannah's father had been ill and he had to borrow some goods to feed his family; but he didn't get better. He died, and his creditors came and took away his children and sold them as slaves to pay for his debts.'

Michael was silent, and then repeated his question.

'I was telling her what old Isaac told us about Joshua, and the sun standing still, and how God can do wonderful things for us.'

'You shouldn't have done that,' he rebuked her sharply. 'You're only a child. What do you know about life? It can be sad and cruel. Hannah may be a slave for the rest of her life and she'll have to make the best of it.'

Joanna was indignant. She chattered on but Michael wasn't listening. He was remembering his mother's obvious distress when they had heard Hannah crying. Now, as he heard the girl's story he was searching his mind. Why was Mother so upset then he asked himself? She had heard the girl crying before. Could it be because she knew that if Father died or couldn't work that the same thing might happen to them, that they might be sold as slaves? Michael tried to shut the thought from his mind. Father was getting better. Abigail didn't say much. She never did, but it was obvious that she was confident that Enoch would walk again.

Yes, certainly, Father's foot was improving. You could see that it was a foot now, though it would be some weeks before he would be able to put it to the ground, but Father himself was not looking better. Instead he seemed to be getting older and greyer as the days passed. The showing of white at his temples when he had first been carried home from the mines was becoming more prominent, and his black beard was tinged with grey. His fine wide forehead was deeply furrowed, and lines creased his sunken cheeks. He had become an old man. And worst of all, their home, which had always been a haven of love and peace, seemed to be filled with discord. Michael couldn't tell exactly what it was but it left him feeling as he had when his cousin had tried to play a lyre that had been strung too tightly.

A month passed and it was time for the harvesting of the grapes. Michael had been trying to suppress his fears and join in his sister's spirit of optimism, but it was a continual battle. One day, as he was entering the house he passed their odious neighbour, Shamei, on his way out, oozing self satisfaction. 'That's right, my boy,' he gushed, patting Michael on the head. 'Work hard now, grow nice and strong,' for all the world as if Michael were a sweet juicy morsel he was waiting to devour. As Michael entered the inner courtyard he could hear his father's voice raised. He thought his mother was in tears, though she tried to hide it from her son.

The vats were fast being filled with the fragrant purple wine, but instead of it being a time for rejoicing, as it usually was, the tension seemed to be mounting. Enoch was struggling about on crutches, though he was forbidden to do so, urging the men on.

'What is it, Mother? Why is Father so worried?' Michael asked , when he had his mother to himself.

'You know, Son. The tax collectors will be here soon. We were given this estate on the understanding that we should supply our quota for the King's table.'

Her answer did not satisfy him. They had never had any trouble in fulfilling their quota before, and the harvest was plentiful this year. There would be the late wheat and barley to harvest next, but there seemed to be the same spirit of anxiety building up over this event too.

Then, one night, as the children lay sleeping on the roof, for it was the dry season and hot winds were blowing from the desert, Michael was awakened by his parents' voices below. He could not hear their words but he knew that their voices were raised, and then he heard his mother sobbing. Michael was determined to get to the bottom of the trouble.

Early the next morning he waylaid his mother as she returned from the well. 'Forgive me, Mother, I must speak to you.'

'There, run along, Joanna,' and she set her pitcher down and walked a little way with her son, her firstborn.

'Mother, I beg of you, do not be vexed, but I must know what is wrong. I am your son. Surely I have a right to know. I could not help but hear you and Father talking last night and I heard you crying. It is more than Father's foot isn't it? Mother, I beseech you to tell me.'

But his Mother could not answer him. Great sobs arose

from deep within her. She pulled her veil over her face and turned from him.

Poor Michael, he might just as well have asked his little sister in the first place, for in the end it was she who told him the cause of their trouble.

CHAPTER FIVE

'That Shamei is a wicked, wicked man,' exploded Joanna, though under her breath, for one never knew when he might come sneaking up. She had been longing to share her burden with her brother, and now, as he had been sent to help her to pluck a fowl, she had the chance for which she had been waiting.

'I know, - I don't trust him at all,' muttered Michael in response. 'But why do you say so? Have you found out something?'

'Yes, I have and, O Michael, it is so terrible! I understand now why Father is so worried, and can't get better. He is in debt to Shamei!'

The boy's hands dropped, his task forgotten. He was speechless. He could understand now his father's feverish anxiety over the harvests.

'But how, Joanna? However did it happen?' he managed to blurt out, but even as he spoke he had a flashback of memory. Shamei - compelling his mother into the inner room - emerging, thrusting something into his robe. 'He made her pledge to pay him for sending those men to carry Father home. That's it, is it not?

Joanna nodded.

How had he not seen it before? 'And he made everyone believe that he was doing it out of neighbourly
kindness!' There was bitterness in his voice.

The vultures had been sitting on a wall nearby, scraggy
necks stretched, hooded eyes watching for the offal
that would be left for them. They saw the carcase now
left unguarded and hopped down strutting nearer. The
children drove them away and resumed their task.

'How did you find out?' Michael whispered.

'I was up on the roof, spreading out the flax. Mother
and Father were talking below me. They didn't
realise I was there. I heard Father say, "Only two vats
short and now we owe four. And it will be the same
with the oil and the wheat and the barley. O Jerusha, if
only you had known, when you signed that paper, you
were signing away your very life's blood! If we cannot
pay he gets our house and estate and we'll all be sold
as slaves." '

'I'm waiting for that chicken, young master,' a
servant called.

They hastily finished their task, wiping away their
tears. Joanna ran with it to the pot while Michael
swept up the feathers - the vultures would clear the
rest - and set off again for the fields, but before he left

his sister returned and clung to him for a moment.

'Michael, we've got to hope in God,' she whispered. 'I know you didn't like me telling Hannah, but I know it was God who sent the old man Isaac to remind us of that story about Joshua, so that we wouldn't despair. God knows about us. I know He does, and He cares. So let's hope, Michael.'

'Thank you, Joanna.' He returned her embrace. 'I'll try.'

As he trudged back to the field where they were harvesting the wheat Michael felt as if his heart had turned to stone within him, but somewhere a bird began to trill and, unbidden, the words of a song of their minstrel King ,David came to him - 'Hope thou in God, for I shall yet praise Him.'

The wheat was all harvested. There were no gleanings left this year. The sacks were set aside ready to be collected to go to Jerusalem for the King's requirements. Once again their scheming neighbour came for his portion. Enoch could have paid him in full but it would have left him without seed for planting, or food for his household. Yet again the debt was increased.

The little family sat around their evening meal of lentil broth and barley cakes. The father bowed his head to give thanks.

'Try to eat, my dear,' Jerusha encouraged her husband. She reached out to pat his hand. 'We want to put some flesh on these bones.'

Michael saw his hand was thin, almost transparent, like that of a skeleton, but he noted that Joanna, still plump for all their hardship, was eating heartily. There seemed to be a brightness in her eye. 'Doesn't she care? Or is it that she is a child and doesn't really understand?' he asked himself, but he knew in his heart that neither supposition was true. Later he realised the cause of the sparkle.

'Father,' she said, 'the Teacher is coming to our town tomorrow. Michael may go, mayn't he?'

'Oh, no, I'd better help with the ploughing,' offered Michael, but he was thankful when his father replied firmly, 'Certainly, Son, you must go!'

Enoch began to recite from a loved psalm. He went through a stanza that he had learned from a Levite who had come to his village in his boyhood. 'Blessed are the undefiled in the way, who walk in the law of the Lord.' He added, 'The Teacher has come at a good time. We can spare you for a day or two. He has a wide circuit, and may not be back here for a year or more. Yes, certainly, my Son, you must go.'

As they went to get out their mat beds for the night Joanna pulled her brother aside. 'Listen, Michael. You are to tell the Teacher about our trouble. I am sure that God is sending him just now to help us.'

'For shame, Joanna,' he interrupted her. 'How could I ever do that?'

'Michael, you must. The Teacher is a Levite, a man of God. I feel sure that God will use him to tell us what to do.'

Michael used to look forward to this brief schooling. The boys of the town would gather in one of the larger courtyards, each of them sprinkling sand on the hard earth floor, and writing on it with his finger according to the Levite's instruction. 'Thou shalt love the Lord thy God....' they wrote. They recited together the ten commandments, and many passages from the law of Moses. Then they would sing some of the psalms of King David. But this time there was something different. Their Teacher brought out a scroll.

'This is new,' he told them proudly. 'It is a book of proverbs compiled by our great King Solomon.' The boys listened, enthralled. 'The fear of the Lord is the beginning of knowledge..' he began. He read on and on.

34

There was one that Michael felt spoke directly to his heart. It went like this. 'Remember the Lord in everything you do, and He will show you the right way.' Show you the right way. Maybe Joanna was right, the man of God would help them, but however could he approach him?

The day passed swiftly. They stood to sing a psalm of praise together, the Teacher gave his blessing, and they were on their way home. But Joanna was waiting for her brother outside the gate.

'Did you ask him, Michael?' she whispered.

'Joanna, go home, you shouldn't be here,' he remonstrated, embarrassed.

But the girl persisted, 'Michael, you must ask him! You must!'

'Ask me what, may I know?' It was the Teacher himself. He stood there, looking down on them, his black eyes twinkling under his bushy eyebrows.

CHAPTER SIX.

The day passed slowly for Joanna as she waited for the evening to come again and for their promised meeting with the Teacher. Eli Ben Hadad had been so kind and understanding. Seeing the tears in the children's eyes, and noting their obvious distress, he had guided them through the wide streets of the town to the house where he was lodging. There was a room there, upon the roof, specially prepared for the visits of men such as he, but it was not there that he took them. He led them instead to the shade of the fig tree where he knew they could talk undisturbed.

Eli had listened gravely, without interrupting, while Michael related the sad sequence of events, from his father's accident in the mines to their present calamity of being in debt and their father's ill health. He made no movement except to twisting together his fingers when he heard of their neighbour's involvement, as if he would have liked to wring his neck.

Joanna tried to sit quietly knowing that it was not her place as a woman to do the talking, but she did speak now and again. 'Michael, you forgot to tell about the old man, Isaac. That was how Abigail came to us.' Or , 'Mother couldn't read of course, and she had no idea to what she was agreeing.'

'Of course, I understand.' The Teacher nodded gravely.

'Like a wise old owl,' Joanna thought.

He sat with his fingers pressed together, his head bowed. Then he turned his keen black eyes upon them. 'Tell me!' he demanded.'Have you any reason to believe that God should help you?'

'Oh, yes sir, yes sir.' It was Joanna who burst out, but he silenced her.

'Michael, you first.'

'Well sir, Joanna has always been telling me that we should believe that God would help us, because of something that happened when we were walking home from Jerusalem after we had heard of Father's accident.This old man joined us...'and he went on to relate the event, and his sister's insistence that this was a sign of hope for them.

'But what about you, Michael?' he probed. 'Your sister's faith is not enough for you. Has God not spoken to you?'

The boy hesitated.He uncrossed his legs, and then crossed them again, tucking his tunic carefully over his knees as he searched his memory. Then his face lit up.

'You know the book you read to us yesterday, sir, the new one, the King's book? There was one of the proverbs that, well, made me hope - like Joanna is always saying.'

'Well?' The Teacher waited.

'It went something like this.' Michael spoke hesitantly. 'Remember the Lord in everything you do,' he began, 'and He will show you the right way,' joined in the Teacher.

'Good, that's enough to assure me that God has an answer in this situation. I will spend time in prayer. Meet me here tomorrow, after the lessons and I am confident that I will have an answer for you. Meanwhile, go in peace.'

Joanna was never idle. There was water to fetch, corn to grind, work in the small field near the house where they grew their vegetables, and she always had to be ready to support her father as he limped around. Then there was spinning and weaving to be done and if she and her mother were working together her mother would instruct her in the laws of Moses concerning their household duties. At last the shadow of the date palm was nearing the house and Joanna knew that it was time to go. She watched for Michael as he came out of school with the other boys.

Letting the Teacher walk on ahead of them, they waited until he was seated under the fig tree and had been refreshed with water, and then they joined him. Eli continued to sit in silence, his head bowed, but at last he looked up. 'I don't understand,' he began slowly, 'but I believe that your father himself has the answer.'

'What do you mean, sir? We assure you that our father is quite unable to clear his debts,' Michael insisted.

'Not with oil or wine, maybe. Perhaps there is something else? Has he something of gold or silver that he could trade to clear his debts?'

The children shook their heads. 'We don't think so.'

'Well, I don't understand, but I believe this is the message I have been given. You must tell your father that the answer lies with him.'

They stood as the Teacher placed his hands on their heads and prayed for them.

They were very quiet as they walked home.

'How can we tell Father that?' complained Michael.

'We'll just have to start at the beginning, how we felt that we had to ask the Teacher to help us,' answered his sister. 'We must tell him, Michael. After all, there is an answer, and that is wonderful.'

'That's right.' Hope began to rise again in his breast. "The answer is with your father." Yes, that's right. There is an answer.'

They waited until they had finished their meal and their father had prayed. 'Father, we have something to tell you ,' Michael began and of course Joanna was soon joining in to relate her part and the story was told. 'He said we were to tell you that the answer is with you.'

Father was indignant. 'Do you think I want to be in debt?' he expostulated. 'Do I want to lose my home and my family?' But the children had noticed an almost guilty look pass between their parents, and Jerusha began to plead, 'O Enoch! Maybe we...' but he had silenced her with 'I don't know what he can mean,' and the conversation was ended.

The children lay awake far into the night. There was an answer, they were convinced of it now, but what could it be? Was it some possession of their father's? What could he possibly have that would be of sufficient value to free them from the terrible burden of their debt?

Before the first light of dawn Michael arose. He must speak with his mother alone, for he was convinced that she knew something.

CHAPTER SEVEN.

Michael did at last manage to speak with his mother alone, as she set out for the well, but she seemed ill at ease, as if she wanted to get away from him.'Your father does have something that is precious to him. He keeps it in a little box. Ask him about it,' was all she would say.

As it turned out Michael didn't have to ask. His brief days of schooling were over now and he found it hard to go back to his labour in the fields. They were preparing for the winter sowing. All day he was turning over in his mind how he could approach his father concerning the box but, having washed and changed his clothing and coming ready for the meal that they always ate together as a family, he saw that his father had a small sandalwood box set on a lampstand close beside him. Could it be that all this time his father had had a precious jewel hidden away, and they in such distress?

'Father,' Michael began, but his parent silenced him with a look. Enoch had to raise his hand to Joanna though, for, in her excitement, she would have run up to touch the box.

'Your mother has prepared a meal for us, my children. We will eat first, and then your curiosity shall be satisfied.' Their father's word was law.

They ate in silence. The prayer was said. At last Enoch took the little box in his hands. 'I have been thinking much about the words of the Teacher,' he began. 'The trouble we are in is through no fault of our own. Our covetous neighbour took advantage of your mother when she was distraught with grief so that she had no idea we would be bound by this impossible commitment. We have struggled to meet it, but all the time we are sinking deeper and deeper into debt. With my accident in the mines and with the burden of this worry I have become broken in spirit and in body. Indeed I fear that I may not live much longer.'

Jerusha, who had been sitting with bowed head, came weeping now and buried her head in her husband's lap. 'But my children are teaching me to hope in God,' he continued. She lifted her face at this and sat up, her eyes upon him. 'I have been thinking and praying about the words of the Teacher. I believe that he is a man of God, and that the message he gave you must have come from God and yet-.' He paused, shaking his head sadly, 'I don't know.'

'Father, what is it? Please show us ?' Joanna could not contain her curiosity. Enoch took the box in his hands. The children were on either side of him, their cheeks pressed against his as they crowded to see.

There, wrapped in a piece of fine linen, was a small white stone. It was beautiful in its snowy whiteness but as Enoch picked it up and held it on the palm of his hand they saw that it had been broken. There were rings of colour within it and the centre part, which was jet black, was ridged segmentally.

'Is it valuable, Father?' questioned Michael, his disappointment apparent.

'I used to think that it was, Michael, but I've been trained as a stone mason and in the skill of mining.No, I know now that it is of no value to anyone else. And yet - yes, it is valuable to me!'

'But Father!' began Joanna. She was near to tears. Had her hopes been raised only to have them dashed again? But Michael sensed that there was something more. He took his sister's hand to pull her down beside him, crossed his legs, then asked, 'Please , Father, tell us?Tell us how it is that you have had this stone hidden away like this. It must have been in a very secret place for we have never seen it before.'

'We had left our village to come and live in Jerusalem,' Enoch began. 'I was only a boy. There was a Syrian who had a field close by the city walls. He had come to breed horses, for they were beginning to be popular then with the rich folk . He employed my father to work for him and I used to go and help too. There was a beautiful foal, black as jet. Kedar, we called it. I had been there when it was born and I would go every day and take it titbits and we would run and play together. There was another boy who loved the foal as I did, and we became friends. I knew that he came from the King's household, that he was one of the princes, but that didn't make any difference to us. Sometimes, if no one was about, we would mount the horses and ride bare back. One day the owner came and shouted at us. My friend galloped straight up to him and proudly declared, 'I am Jedidiah, son of King David. My friend and I would like to exercise your horses for you from time to time. If you need recompense, my father will see to it.'

So, from then on we often rode out together. One day we were cantering through some forest land when we surprised a wild sow with her litter. We didn't hurt her, and we watched quietly while she trotted off, her piglets squealing after her, but we couldn't explain this to the old boar. We should have known that he would be around, of course, but he caught us unawares. Grunting with rage, it gouged a hole in the side of Jedidiah's horse and brought it to the ground. There would have been a sad ending to the story if there hadn't been two of us, but I galloped up shouting and screaming and diverted the beast's attention so that my friend could get to his feet.'

'Oh Father!' exclaimed Joanna, breathless with excitement. 'Did you kill the boar?'

'No,' Enoch laughed. 'We were younger than you are, Joanna, and we weren't armed.'

'But you both lived to tell the tale, didn't you, Father? Is this the meaning of the stone?'

'Yes, Michael. I saw that my friend had scrambled up a tree for safety and then I rode for help. The next day he showed me this white stone, beautiful, like a pigeon's egg. We took it to the smith and he broke it for us. It fell into two perfect halves. We were delighted at the way it broke, with this beautiful segmentation. It fitted so perfectly together. We both took a nail and inscribed our initials on our own half and then we exchanged them.

'We're friends now for always and always, and we'll always help each other,' we promised.

'Father, Father, that's wonderful.' Joanna was dancing round the room in her delight. 'He's a prince. He'll be able to help us. He'll pay the debt for us. Everything will be all right and you'll get well and strong again.' She flung her arms around her father's neck, but Michael was more practical.

'Father?' he asked, 'Who is this Prince Jedidiah? Is he dead, or has he gone away? I've never heard of him.'

'No,' replied his father, shaking his head sadly.'You have never heard of him because he goes by another name now. When I tell you, you will realise why it is that I have not felt that I could claim his promise or go to him for help. Jedidiah is King Solomon.'

CHAPTER EIGHT

The boy looked a lonely figure as he made his way once more through the valley of Ajalon. The stone was safely in his keeping. Maybe it was just an ordinary piece of quartz, such as might be chanced upon on any beach, but it was a stone of infinite worth should it be honoured by the holder of its counterpart.

The children had had to plead long with their parents before they had been willing for Michael to make this journey, to the city and the King, for, of course, it was out of the question for Enoch to go.

'Why should the great King Solomon be concerned about a small boy that he used to play with?' his father had reasoned.'You could incur his wrath for your effrontery in approaching the throne of judgment. The wrath of the King is something very terrible.'

Michael had felt the blood draining from his body as once again they spoke of the awful throne of judgment. It was Joanna who had brought them back to their present plight.

'Father, don't you see? We've got nothing to lose. If we go on as we are ,we will be separated as a family. Michael will be conscripted for the King's work force. He could end up full time in the mines and we would never see him again. And what of Mother and me?' Tears ran down her face as she clung to her mother and they wept together.

Enoch sat in silence. At last he spoke.'Fetch me the stone, Michael.' They all knew now the secret of its hiding place, behind a loose brick beside the alcove where they stored their bed rolls. Placing it in a soft leather pouch he showed his son how to conceal it on his body.'Let no one see it, no one at all, until you show it to the King.'

Michael had left by the first chill light of dawn, for it was winter. 'No sun for Joshua to command even,' was his thought as he entered the valley, recalling old Isaac and how he had intruded into their grief to remind them of the story. The lad remembered it all so clearly. At that time his mother had been overwhelmed by fear because of her husband's accident and yet now his foot was healing. This had become the least of their worries.

Searching back through his memory, he came upon his mother's seemingly unreasonable distress at hearing the wail of the little slave girl. It could only have been because of her fear that a like calamity would fall upon them. Could it be, Michael pondered, that her fears had somehow drawn these calamities upon them?

An icy rain began to beat upon him. He knew that Isaac's house was nearby and decided to run there for shelter. He would not disclose the secret of the stone but would tell them only that his father had entrusted him with a message for the King.

Abigail threw some brushwood onto the fire they had burning in an open hearth in the centre of their mud-walled house. Her husband was glad of the rain, which gave him an excuse to sit and warm his old bones, and especially as it had driven in someone else to lend him a listening ear, for Isaac loved to talk.

'Joshua defeated the Amorites,' he began after enquiring about the family. 'King David defeated the Philistines. King Solomon has made treaties of peace with all the nations that used to oppress us. But we still have enemies, you know.' It was as though he was talking to himself.

'Yes, I do know,' thought Michael. 'That old Shamei is our enemy all right.'

'But our worst enemies are within us,' Isaac went on. Michael was brought back from Shamei. What could Isaac mean?

'You think now,' he continued, seeing he had the boy's interest. 'Think of your trouble. It isn't so much what your neighbour has done to your father. It is your father's worry and fear and resentment that is making him weak and ill.'

'It isn't so easy to fight against enemies like that, enemies that you can't see, is it?' questioned Michael.

'But I see that you are fighting.' A smile broke over the old man's wrinkled face. 'Trust in God. That's the best weapon against those enemies.'

'Remember the Lord in everything you do, and He will show you the right way.' Michael repeated his favourite proverb.

'That's it! That's it, my boy!' He clapped Michael on the back. They were on their feet now for Abigail had just called to them that the shower was over.

There were not many people about and Michael was glad when at last he had turned onto the main highway. A watery sun broke through the clouds and there in the distance he could see it-Jerusalem, City of Peace. For a moment the glistening white of the temple was lit up as it towered majestically over the old city, houses huddled around it.

Michael made his way in through the great gate and up through the narrow streets where he and Jonadab, yes and the girls too, had scampered in such carefree abandon just a few months ago. 'I was a child then,' he thought. Another year and he would be twelve. His father, if he lived, would bring him to the temple for the Passover festival and he would be received into the community as a man. 'Yet, I am a man now,' he thought, for a great weight of responsibility had been laid upon him.

Once again he stood at the great wall of the temple as it towered above him. Surely the impossible had been accomplished in the hewing out of those colossal stones. Why, some weighed as much as a hundred tons, his father had told him, yet the builders had had faith and courage to do it. The temple would stand there, through all generations, as a testimony to their faith in God.

Michael made his way to the front of the temple, marvelling at the two great pillars, Jachin and Boaz, with their wondrous carvings, all overlayed with gold, but it was not here he would find the King. He continued upward a little toward the north of the city where the new development was taking place. He wondered at the fine houses of stone and marble, but the palace, built of cedar wood, put all else in the shade. It was a masterpiece of architectural magnificence, and yet, Michael did not thrill to its beauty. A heavy rain was falling again and a chill seemed to be soaking through his body to his very heart, for the great iron gates to the palace were shut and soldiers, spears at the ready, stood on guard.

'How, oh how am I going to be able to get in to see the King?' Michael did not feel like a man now. He was just a small boy, cold and wet and alone.

CHAPTER NINE

The next morning the gates were open and the palace courtyard was a blaze of activity. As Michael drew near, a chariot from some Eastern court swept through to receive a royal welcome. The boy approached with confidence, for was he not on a visit to the childhood companion of his father, the two pledged in eternal friendship? As he made to go through the gates, however, there was a clash of steel. Two guards held their spears aslant, barring his way, while the hand of another gripped him by the shoulder.

'Now then, young fellow. Where do you think you are going? None of your cheek now!'

'But, sir, if you please, sir, I have a message for the...' but before Michael could finish he had been flung roughly aside. He tried to regain his composure and again he drew near, but this time the spear was pointed into his chest.

'Be off with you now!'

Michael had spent the night at the house of his cousin, Jonadab. Eagerly they had listened to his news of the family at Amwas. They had wept with him as they heard of Enoch's sorry state when he was carried home from the mines, ejaculated in anger over Shamei's double dealings, and sighed in wonder over the revelation that Enoch actually had a claim on King Solomon, though, of course, Michael did not disclose the truth of the precious burden that he bore.

'Oh Michael,' his aunt encouraged him, 'surely you are going to the only one who can help you. Our great King has brought peace into our troubled land, and he will surely bring justice into your situation. Why, who has not heard of the wisdom of the judgments of Solomon?' But the boy who had left them that morning, his courage so high, stood now wounded, not so much by his physical manhandling, as by the indignity of the way he had been treated. He dusted himself down, turned aside to find a water carrier for a refreshing drink, then squatted down in a quiet alley where he could see yet not be seen.

'I've got to get to King Solomon,' he affirmed to himself. 'I've got to get past those guards and into the palace. I must. If only I can get to him and show him the stone, my mission is accomplished.'

Michael walked around the palace walls until he came to another entrance, but this was made equally secure. He tried to gain admittance there but, 'Visitors at the main entrance, *if* you please,' and guffaws of raucous laughter followed him as he walked on.

It was a dejected boy who returned to his cousin's home that night. He was so grateful for the bowl of broth they shared with him.

'When the guards were changed I approached again,' he related, 'but they were all the same. They seemed to think it was the chance for some sport. One man really twisted my arm.'

'I've some mustard oil. I'll massage it for you,' his aunt soothed.

'There must be some way to get in,' Jonadab pondered. 'Or if not, the King is sure to come out.'

'Yes, call out to him as he drives out. Tell him that you have a message for him.' It was his uncle's suggestion.

So it was that Michael set out the next day with fresh courage. He did not approach the palace gates at once but waited quietly, out of sight of the guards. Noon passed, and Michael ran down one street and up another to warm himself. He returned just in time to glimpse a chariot, gleaming with gold, drawn by four magnificent black stallions, driving out through the gates. It was Solomon, the King.

'My Lord the King!' His young voice rang out clearly

above the clatter of the hooves. 'I have a message for the King.' None hearkened or heeded. His voice had no more significance than the chirping of the sparrows upon the palace roof.

Later in the day an embassage approached the gates. Some dark beauty was carried in, in an ornate palanquin. Attendants followed, laden with gifts for the King. Michael thought he might slip in amongst them but he was easily recognised by the guards by now.

'You're very anxious to see the King, young fellow,' the guard who held him remarked, not unkindly.

'I have a message for him, sir. A message from his friend.'

'A message for him, eh?' The soldier shook his head. 'I'm afraid our King Solomon is too busy with all his friends from foreign parts these days. I don't think there is too much chance of him having time to listen to a message from his friend.'

'It's true,' his fellow guard joined in. 'There was a time when any of his people could approach him and be sure of a hearing. Maybe he has become too great a King.'

'On your way now, lad!' his captor commanded, kindly this time. He turned the boy around and gave

him a push, away from the palace. 'Best go home, my
lad!'

Michael's eyes were brimming with tears. It felt as if
he had a stone instead of a heart within his
breast.'Remember the Lord..' He tried to repeat his
special proverb, but somehow it had lost its power to
lift his spirits. 'Is there a right way to reach the King?'
he asked himself. 'I know ,that if only I can reach him
to show him the stone ,that everything will be all right.'
He thought about Joshua, standing outside the city of
Jericho, so long ago. That was an impregnable city,
they said, its walls so thick that a chariot could drive
upon them. But Joshua got in. The walls had fallen
down flat. Then , there was this very city, the city of
Jerusalem. The Jebusites, who lived there, had looked
over the ramparts, mocking at King David. 'You'll
never take this city,' they jeered. 'Why, the lame and
the blind could hold it against you.' But the King sent
his men up the water course. They got in, and David
took the city.

'Then surely, surely, there is a way for me to get past
those guards and to see the King,' Michael thought.
'Remember the Lord in everything you do, and He will
show you the right way.'

At last evening came. The palace gates were closed.
Cold and disconsolate, Michael was glad to escape to

the security of his cousin's home. 'Perhaps I should give up,' he thought. 'But how can I go home without having even shown the King the white stone?'

But Jonadab had news for him. 'Michael, do you remember Joanna's friend, Deborah? She came here today to visit my mother. We told her about you and she thinks that she may be able to help.'

Deborah! Michael searched his memory. Yes - the patter of feet following them as they had scampered so carefree through the streets of Jerusalem, - a girl, shy, but with a queenly tilt to her head, a tint of fire in her dark hair and admiration shining in her amber eyes. Yes, he remembered Deborah, but - how could she help?

'You see, Michael, her mother has recently been asked to attend the Queen.'

CHAPTER TEN

Queen Bathsheba sat at her spinning wheel. Graciously she turned and motioned to Michael to come and sit on a stool beside her. He was grateful for the warmth of the fire that was glowing in a brazier nearby. 'I think perhaps we would appreciate being alone,' she smiled at Deborah's mother, who had brought the lad to her there. She, and the other women who were the Queen's companions, quietly slipped away.

Michael's first impression had been of an old woman as he saw the Queen Mother bowed over her distaff, for her hair was lightened by silver threads, but as she turned toward him, he was aware of the freshness of her cheeks and he looked into eyes that were still pools of beauty.

'Now then, Michael,' she began, 'I hear that you desire an audience with the King. Perhaps I can help you, I don't know, but if you want me to try to help you then you must take me as your friend and confide in me. Will you do that, lad?'

'Oh Madam!' Michael, touched by her gentle kindness, felt his eyes fill with tears, as he flung himself at her feet, but she lifted him up so that he was once again seated on the stool.

'Tell me, first of all, how it is that you know my lady in waiting, Anna, for she tells me that you are come from Amwas.'

'I don't really know her, Madam. My mother brought us to Jerusalem to visit her sister, while my father was away for his month of duty. He is a skilled engineer, and had been sent to the new copper mine. While we were here, my sister Joanna became friendly with Anna's daughter, Deborah.'

'And so you became friends?' The Queen leaned forward, her eyes twinkling.

'Yes..no..!' Michael was embarrassed. 'You see, it was the day the Queen of Sheba arrived in Jerusalem,' he began, and went on to tell the whole story. He didn't get it all in the right order, and now and again Bathsheba interrupted, to make sure that she understood.

When Michael came to the story of his father's friendship with her son, Solomon, she seemed enthralled.

'I remember, yes, Jedidiah - it was later he wanted to be called Solomon - often went to the stables. He has always loved horses. I remember him telling me about the foal. "Mother, I beg you, ask my father to buy it for me. I want it for my very own." '

'Did you?' Michael asked.

'I did,' she sighed. 'I don't know if I was kind in always doing what he asked. But - yes, I remember him telling me about the boar, but I didn't know that it was your father who saved him.' She turned back to her spinning wheel and for a few moments twisted and spun the thread, as if to prevent any interruption to her thoughts, then turned again to the boy.

'Michael,' she asked gently, 'may I see the stone?'

Reluctantly he pulled out the leather pouch that was hidden under his robe then, tipping the precious token on to his palm, he held it out to her. Bathsheba did not pick it up straight away but, holding Michael's rough hand in both of her soft ones, gazed at this token, a part of her now famous son's childhood.

At last she spoke. 'Michael, would you trust me with this stone? Would you trust me to present it to the King?'

The boy closed his hands over the stone and bowed his head a moment, then, pressing the stone into her's, again he prostrated himself at her feet.

'Queen Bathsheba,' he murmured softly as he rose, 'our lives are in your hands.' He rose to go, a song of joy in his heart but, motioning him back to his stool the Queen clapped her hands. 'Come!' she called, 'Refreshment!'

Girls, about Deborah's age, brought in dishes of honey cakes and fruit and set them beside Michael. As the doors were left open, the sound of a harp flowed into the room. Someone was letting his fingers wander idly over the strings, and then a man began to sing. It was not a song of jubilation as the boy had expected, but rather a lament. His voice was low and soft.

'Why are You so far away, O Lord?' It was one of King David's songs, about all the people who are oppressed and in trouble. 'The wicked are proud and persecute the poor.' He crashed out a discord on the harp. 'He hides himself in the villages, waiting to murder innocent people.'

'Why was he singing this terrible song, just when I thought all our troubles were going to be over?' Michael was ill at ease. 'Why does she keep me here? I don't belong here. I want to go home.'

The Queen was obviously distressed by the song too. She signalled to her attendants. They quietly slipped away, the doors closed behind them. The harpist had been silenced. Once more Michael was alone with the Queen. She walked around the room, evidently in some agitation, then came and held out to him the pouch containing the white stone. Michael couldn't believe that this was happening. Had his hopes been raised, only to be dashed again? Was this beautiful lady playing with him, saying that she would help him and then changing her mind? 'Hope! Hope in God!' That was what he had been told. How could he hope now? Unwillingly he took the stone from her.

'My son, forgive me?' Bathsheba's voice was soft and low. 'Yes, it is true, I am the Queen Mother. I could go to my son and intercede for you. But, don't you see, you aren't the only family in trouble.'

Michael's thoughts flashed back to the little slave girl back in their own town, weeping as she collected the dung.

'It's a disgrace that you have had to be brought to me, for you should be able to go directly to your King. Every one of his subjects should be able to approach him.'

'Oh, but Madam, I tried. Truly, I have tried and tried.' Once again the tears sprang up as he thought of his humiliation at the palace gates. She touched his shoulder lightly, expressing her understanding and compassion.

'Listen, my son, I have a plan. If you will have courage, and do as I say, I believe that you will find help not only for your own family, but for many people in this realm.'

CHAPTER ELEVEN

The boy trembled as he waited, hiding behind a pillar in the covered way between the palace and the temple. The guard must surely hear the sound of his knees knocking together. The palms of his hands were clammy and his tongue felt as if it were stuck to the roof of his mouth. However would he be able to utter a sound if the King did come?

An unearthly screech sounded from somewhere over the palace wall. 'It's all right,' mouthed the guard, standing close by. 'Just one of those peacocks the Queen of Sheba presented to the King.' A clang echoed up the passageway as someone prepared to open the gates that led from the palace.

It was Queen Bathsheba who had put Michael in the care of the guard, asking him to hide the boy there. She knew that there he could not fail to have an opportunity to approach the King, as he would make his way into the temple for his morning devotions. 'I hope she is still in favour with her son,' the man grumbled to himself, 'or they'll be looking for someone else to fit my uniform.'

Michael realised only too well that he was taking a terrible risk, but he remembered his father and the family at home: the evil Shamei, like a vulture, waiting to devour them. If the King was in an angry mood; if he didn't even get the chance to show him the white stone, what then? The King wasn't likely to have him killed when he was in need of so many labourers for his task forces. No, he might be sent away as a slave, to labour full time - maybe up in the copper mines. But he could end up there anyway if he didn't make his petition to the King. He fumbled, almost dropping the precious token, as he struggled to take it out of its pouch. He clasped it firmly in his hand.

A trumpet heralded the entrance of Solomon the magnificent. Michael was aware of a robe ablaze with embroidery of silver and pearls, of hands dripping with jewels, but he dare not lift his eyes higher. 'It's now or never, my lad,' muttered the guard, and pushed him out.

'My Lord, the King!' Once again his boyish treble rang out and once again the guards sprang upon him. He was held firmly between them.

'I claim the right..' Michael tried to continue, but a slap across the mouth silenced him.

'What is the meaning of this?' blazed the King. 'Can I not even go into the temple of the Lord without being interrupted? Are my guards unable to protect my privacy?'

The one who had hidden Michael there stepped forward. 'If it please your majesty, it is I who am responsible.'

The guards holding Michael drew their swords and turned on him, but the King held out his hand to stay them.

'Your mother, the gracious Queen Bathsheba, asked me to bring the lad here, so that he might have the chance to approach you.'

'But why here, when I go to prayer? Surely here, of all places, I should not be disturbed. Why did he not come to me in the palace?'

'Sire, for three days he stood without, seeking to gain an entrance.'

Solomon turned to look at this lad who was so persistent in seeking to reach him. His face was white, and his dark eyes, uplifted to him now, were wide with fear but, released from the grip of the soldiers, he stepped forward and knelt before the King.

'Your Majesty, I claim the right as one of your subjects, to present my petition to you.'

Michael's young voice rang out like a clarion. His words were those the Queen had counselled him to use. Each one of the King's attendants heard him. The King could not turn him away now.

Solomon turned to his minister of state. 'I sit in judgment tomorrow, at the eighth hour. See that the lad is presented to me.'

* * * * * * *

'I was afraid when I was hiding in the covered way meeting the King with just a few of his attendants, but now I had to face him in the full splendour of his court,' said Michael when he was recounting the story to his sister, for she wanted to hear it over and over again.

'I was bathed and perfumed, and dressed in a robe of fine linen. When I was led into the throne room I knew that it was full of people. There was a low murmur of voices, but I was only conscious of the throne and of the one who sat upon it. Then someone gave me a push. "Go on, Michael! They are all waiting for you. Go on! Don't be afraid!" It was Deborah - do you remember her?'

'Of course I remember her,' replied Joanna. 'She is my friend. If I had not brought her with us that day we saw the Queen of Sheba she wouldn't have known you and you would never have got to see the King. But go on, Michael!'

'I didn't know where she came from or how she was there, but I was so glad to feel the strength of her support. Somehow I managed to walk across the room. The gold of the throne was gleaming in the afternoon sunlight, the jewels embedded in it flashing, dazzling me in their brilliance, and all I was holding was a piece of quartz. I knelt down when I reached the bottom step of the throne and pressed my face to the ground. I felt as if I could never lift my eyes to look into the face of this mighty monarch.'

'Go on,' Joanna pleaded, though she knew the story now as well as her brother.

'Then all the voices of the people were hushed, and the air was filled with the sound of the singing of birds. It was coming from the throne itself. Then this too died away and a minister called out, "Rise, and state your petition!"

'I thought, this is my father's friend, and so I dared to look up and I called out, "I have a gift to present to the King." The one who had spoken approached to take it from me......'

'Yes, and you called out, loud and clear, "It is for the hand of the King alone,"' interrupted his sister.

'Go on, Joanna, you know the story as well as I do,' admonished Michael.

But his sister pressed her hands together in token of her apology. 'Please go on, Michael. I want to hear it again. It helps me to believe. I know that the King will come to help us.'

'I don't know where I got the strength from, but I called this out, and then the King must have signalled his consent for I was told to approach.

'Approach - up those awesome steps, past the lions of gold that looked as though they might reach out and devour me, through the orchard of jewel-bearing trees, - it was from there that the sound of the singing of the birds had come. I felt as if I had a sledge hammer pounding in my breast, but I stepped right up, lifting up my eyes to look into the face of the King.

'I bring a gift, O King, from your friend.' I spoke quietly now, for him alone to hear, and I placed the stone right in the palm of King Solomon.'

'Tell me what he said,' interrupted Joanna again.

'He gazed at the stone for a long time, and then at last he spoke. "This is a precious gift," he said, "a stone of great worth. Tell me, my boy, how is it that you have it?"

'Then I told him, "It is my father's. His foot was crushed in an accident in the mines and he was unable to bring it himself."

'And you told him father's name,' Joanna persisted. She wanted reassurance.

'Yes, I told him. He asked me, "What is you father's name?" and I replied, "Enoch ben Zerah. He has an estate in the new town of Amwas." And he replied, "Tell your father, I thank him for his gift." '

'That was all. Then they led me away, and there was nothing to do but to return home but, - well, Joanna, what have we gained? I have seen the King, yes. I have parted with the stone in which we had placed so much faith, but we have no assurance, no promise that the King will help.'

'But Michael,' agonised his sister. She didn't know how boys could be so pessimistic. 'Michael, don't you see? You reached the throne.'

CHAPTER TWELVE

The sun had emerged from the tent of night, leaping with exultation into the heavens, proclaiming to the whole world that this, of all days, was a very special day. The olive trees were in bloom, making the countryside around a celebration. Surely the little family at Amwas should have known, but their hearts were heavy, faint through disappointment, and when a stranger came to the gate, asking for Enoch Ben Zerah, Joanna led him straight up the stairs to where her father was sitting. She did not even offer him water, let alone wine. 'Probably someone else come to see about the taxes,' she thought, and returned to her task of grinding the corn.

Joanna had been so sure that King Solomon would come. She had often stood gazing up the road to see if she could see him galloping up in a chariot of gold, drawn by horses of Arabia, bedecked in their finery. He would stride in, in all his majesty, to embrace his old friend. Their enemy, Shamei, would be brought cringing to his feet to receive the King's judgment, while she and Michael would be called to have gifts lavished upon them. For the first few weeks she had arisen early, sweeping out every corner, filling the house with sweet herbs, trying to rally the failing courage of her family. 'He may come today,' she told them.

Michael tried to believe Joanna was right. He had reached the throne. In giving him the stone he had presented the King's own promise back to him. Their King was good. Was he not God's gift to their nation, for had he not brought peace and security to the troubled land of Israel? Yes, he was good. Everyone had heard of the wisdom of his judgments, but - if only he had said something. He hadn't said he would come. But he had made the promise. They had promised to help each other, but of course he was only a lad at the time.

Rhythmically Michael filled his hand with the precious seed and scattered it out in a wide sweep over the field that he was sowing. His thoughts went back to old Isaac in the valley of Ajalon, how he had encouraged them to trust in God. Then there was the wonderful promise in the proverb that Eli the Levite had taught them: 'Remember the Lord in everything you do and He will teach you the right way.' He repeated it now to encourage himself. Surely that had been the right way, finding that Father had had that special stone. There was none other like it in the whole world. No one else had a claim on the King as they had.

And Father had consented. That had been a victory in itself, Enoch allowing his son to go in his place, and after that - so many obstacles to overcome. His mind went back to his long vigil and humiliation outside the palace. But then Deborah - surely it was the Lord who had brought her to his cousin's house that day, and the gentle Queen Bathsheba helping him. Yes, he had reached, and not only reached, he had ascended the throne. 'Hope! Hope!' his heart told him as he turned to cover a fresh section of the field. They would be following now with the plough to turn the seeds into the soil.

It was three months now since Michael had parted with the precious stone and his heart had become sick with disappointment. He was weary with seeing the pain in his father's eyes and noting his increasing weakness. And their poor, dear mother. She had never been able to forgive herself for allowing them to become in debt to the wicked Shamei. Her hair had turned white with worry and sometimes they had found her running round the house, wringing her hands and talking to herself. 'No, of course Mother isn't losing her mind,' Michael had assured Joanna when she had approached him, but in his heart he wasn't so sure.

Doves were cooing from the treetops, the fragrance from the vineyards was wafted towards them and the olives reached out their branches in the breeze like maidens dancing at a wedding. 'Rejoice! Rejoice!' all nature proclaimed, but the hearts of the children were weary with longing and they did not hear.

'Joanna,' Enoch called. 'Bring wine and fruit for our visitor, and call your brother from the field.' The girl did not notice that there was a brightness in her father's voice that she had not heard for a long time. She ran out to the fields.

'Michael,' she called, 'Father wants you. He has a visitor.'

'Is it..?' he began, but then hope turned to fear. 'Probably they have come to conscript me for the King's task force.'

Father and the visitor sat on stools, while Mother and the children were cross-legged on the floor.

'This gentleman has come to see if he can help us concerning our debt,' was Enoch's introduction.

Michael noted the plain, well worn sandals, the robe of a working man, but as he looked into his eyes he knew that he had seen him before.

'First, I would speak to you, my daughter,' the stranger began, and he reached down and took the mother's toil-worn hand in his own smooth one. 'You have been blaming yourself for the trouble that has come to your family, but I want you to know that if this transaction were brought before the King's judgment seat it would not be found binding, for you were tricked into committing yourself to a payment this man had no right to ask. It was his obligation as a neighbour to help you in your distress. So know that you are not condemned, my daughter. Cast off your cares.'

The hand that he had reached out to her was wet now with her tears. Embarrassed, she wiped it with a tress of her hair and wiping it, kissed it reverently.

'And you, Enoch.' He turned now to him.'You were assigned this estate as a reward for your services, but instead of a blessing it has become a burden to you. But you are a skilled craftsman, with great experience. The King has need of such as you in Jerusalem to serve as a consultant in his building projects. And as for your children, we have need of youth such as theirs to serve in the palace.'

The hearts of the young ones leapt for joy. Once again Michael's thoughts flashed back to Deborah who, with Joanna, had scampered through the streets of Jerusalem with them to see the Queen of Sheba. Yes, he would like to go to live in Jerusalem, the City of Peace. But the stranger was continuing.

'As for this estate, I think that we should recommend that it be given to your neighbour, Shamei.'

Joanna had been sitting gazing, wondering at this man who seemed to be able to speak the mind of the King, but now she could no longer be silent.

'Oh, but sir! He is a wicked man. He doesn't deserve it.'

'Peace! Peace, little daughter!' the stranger soothed her. 'You see, your father should not have any more worry. We want him to get strong again. And - the taxes on this estate are to be raised.'

Joanna understood now. How wise, how good was this man. He would give Shamei what he had been coveting all this time, but in gaining his desired possession he would learn to suffer as he had made them suffer. Maybe they could ask him to do something to help Hannah too. She turned to look at her brother. He had not said a word, but there had been a glow on his face ever since he had entered the room and looked into the face of their visitor.

'Michael,' she whispered, 'Is it King Solomon who has sent this gentleman to us?'

'Joanna - this is the King!'

'Yes, my children,' Enoch joined in, 'this is your King, King Solomon.' Then they all bowed low at his feet but, laughing, he made them rise and seat themselves again.

'But today I have come to you as Jedidiah, your father's boyhood friend.'

He held out his hand and there, on his opened palm they saw it - the stone, smooth and white and lustrous, like a pigeon's egg - not a broken half, but the whole.

'Enoch, my friend.' His arm was around him. 'How glad I am that you took me at my word.'

The
High Hill

Pauline Lewis

Biblical novel set in the time of Elijah with its central event being the encounter between Elijah and the prophets of Baal on Mt. Carmel. The story is about Nathan and Anna who know that one day they will be married since it has been arranged by their respective parents.

Read how their faith in God is tested in these stirring times.

for 10-15 years

80pp   *pocket paperback*

ISBN 1 871676 142